JAPAN ANGELS

エンジェルに関している詩

Stean Anthony

YAMAGUCHI SHOTEN

山口書店　京都

Kanji on the cover is the character for angel

Tenshi

Hear my voice at:
<http://www35.tok2.com/home/stean2/>

JAPAN ANGELS
©2019 Stean Anthony
Author's profits
See end of book for details
PRINTED IN JAPAN

Japan Angel

Hat, long nose, right eye

In light armor

Under the heaven-roof

Thy mouth sing

Harvest be

Abundant this good year

JAPAN ANGELS
Contents

Preface		9
1.	Overlooking with unaltered love	11
2.	The white pheasant is a red bird	12
3.	Principal person facing all ways	13
4.	All I need to know for life is here	14
5.	High heels on the bright cloud above	15
6.	Healthy bitter green leaves	16
7.	High mountain snow speaks	17
8.	There she is beneath the wave	18
9.	Learning the words from my teacher	19
10.	Dawn in Kyoto the streets empty	20
11.	Leaping laughing shouting roaring	21
12.	At the top your hand slips into mine	22
13.	My angels run the fire around	23
14.	He turned his head as I approached	24
15.	Over and again I borrow another	25
16.	Searching for thee street by street	26
17.	Prim and smart the officer stands	27
18.	They move in perfect unison	28
19.	Hefting sandbags to flood banks	29
20.	Cold street in the early morning	30
21.	Voices clash & bell the struggle be	31
22.	Check the pigeon-hole again	32
23.	Head to toe in laundered white	33
24.	There's an oil-spill blazing on deck	34
25.	Dark blue shirt, thermometer	35
26.	Looked at from an angle below	36
27.	Power up the turbos mighty roar	37
28.	In the trough behind the wave	38
29.	High walls around them of small jars	39
30.	A path for the mighty	40
31.	Caught my eye as I ran by	41
32.	He held me in his powerful arms	42
33.	Bagged it & smiled me through	43

34.	Closed my hand about you	44
35.	Small beneath he struck the cloud	45
36.	Wings uplift ascending cranes	46
37.	Eye to eye she peered deep	47
38.	Am I really a man or a woman	48
39.	The best lesson I was given	49
40.	Strangely good you walk around	50
41.	Sit on the verandah	51
42.	Under your skirt we beat the chill	52
43.	Quiet there he is behind the tree	53
44.	Accurately describing the form	54
45.	I sat and listened for an hour	55
46.	Compacted clouds two naked babes	56
47.	Call the mountain	57
48.	A valiant strength in your hope	58
49.	Opening now	59
50.	I would prefer not to lick you	60
51.	Humanity must live within Nature	61
52.	Wearing winter plumage	62
53.	Swing the body round the corner	63
54.	Please a special request I know I've been slacking	64
55.	Why are we so happy? Look	65
56.	Keep the gifts of dance & song alive	66
57.	Wings and eyebrows	67
58.	Go from a door to an island	68
59.	The big one will speak	69
60.	White & red together	70
61.	There's a tree with bells	71
62.	One for you & one for me	72
63.	Light on the mountain pure white	73
64.	Look on the water from the hill	74
65.	Trundling down the street	75
66.	At the going-in and coming-out	76
67.	Other-worldly mountain	77
68.	Mellow, sweet and fragrant	78
69.	Future family send me a helper	79
70.	Love will make the world weep	80
71.	Choose the best for Japan	81

72.	Sweet cherub staring at me	82
73.	Wash force through crevice	83
74.	Hard durance lifting leaden feet	84
75.	The hot water pours from the faucet	85
76.	Soft & moist in my hands	86
77.	Ocean currents build and flow	87
78.	Will they be found there	88
79.	Whisper in my finger tips	89
80.	Soundlessly the hands dance	90
81.	Long flight and weary arrival	91
82.	Crowding into screen Nausicaa	92
83.	I took all my clothes off, wooden bowl	93
84.	Lift up high the fingers go	94
85.	Gentle and considerate	95
86.	Pushing the limit within	96
87.	Tight or squashy	97
88.	The way the word the life	98
89.	A dream-song echoing	99
90.	Mukogawa flower anew	100
91.	Hammering the air overhead	101
92.	Long white line setting west	102
93.	Mirror in the gloss	103
94.	A ringing voice the shamisen thrum	104
95.	Warmth presses on me	105
96.	Clanging a bright red stampede	106
97.	Bells going off bong bong bong bong	107
98.	Shoveling the black powder	108
99.	Burning three days three nights	109
100.	The cloth of the sky shaken	110

Notes on the Poems	112
Profile	115
Author's Profits	116
Books by Stean Anthony	117

Preface

This is an anthology of short poems on the theme of angels. I should say straightaway that this is not a book about angels in the Christian, Judaic or Islamic traditions, though it is connected to and inspired by those three traditions. What do I mean by angels?

Japan Angels 1

**Overlooking with unaltered love
Ten thousand years
In their station of highest good**

Japan Angels 2

The white pheasant is a red bird
Prosperity
Shine on the peace-maker Japan

Japan Angels 3

Principal person facing all ways

Happiness given

Season to season continue in joy

Japan Angels 4

All I need to know for life is here
Trust & love
Day by day to learn and grow

Japan Angels 5

High heels on the bright cloud above

Descending

Ascending on the arm of the good one

Japan Angels 6

Healthy bitter green leaves

Thy face beauty

Inspire me goodness strange

Japan Angels 7

High mountain snow speaks
A river thaws
Runs in the sunlight the stream

Japan Angels 8

There she is beneath the wave

Mother

She's floating in the distant sky

Japan Angels 9

Learning the words from my teacher
Love evolving
あいうえお   each stroke   each curve

Japan Angels 10

Dawn in Kyoto the streets empty
The city quiet
A cool breeze along the Kamo

Japan Angels 11

Leaping laughing shouting roaring
Grisly shaking
Stamping yelling   Fling the beans!

Japan Angels 12

At the top your hand slips into mine

Waaay

Down we go and up we go wha hae

Japan Angels 13

My angels run the fire around

Purify the land

I am the torch you're carrying

Japan Angels 14

He turned his head as I approached
And gurned
My innards lurched & I fled in fear

Japan Angels 15

Over and again I borrow another
Shyly glance
O she burns so bright before me

Japan Angels 16

Searching for thee street by street
Where are you
Trusty friend you call my name

Japan Angels 17

Prim and smart the officer stands

Blue & white

In her hands thy safety is assured

Japan Angels 18

They move in perfect unison

Cool elegant

Passion inflames me for them

Japan Angels 19

Hefting sandbags to flood banks
Landslips
Patient heroes digging the earth

Japan Angels 20

Cold street in the early morning

A billow of steam

The maker with hair in a white cap

Japan Angels 21

Voices clash & bell the struggle be

Thy loyal heart

Ware the outer strike the inner demon

Japan Angels 22

Check the pigeon-hole again

By the window

Sit and read what she wrote

Japan Angels 23

Head to toe in laundered white

Soft straw sandals

Hey Ho along the path we grow

Japan Angels 24

There's an oil-spill blazing on deck
In silver space-suits
Hazard-training 1st-years fire-fight

Japan Angels 25

Dark blue shirt, thermometer
Little boy
I'm too busy to play with you

Japan Angels 26

Looked at from an angle below
Fully bright
You seem very glad to see me

Japan Angels 27

Power up the turbos mighty roar

Thunder roll

Forward speed a great one leaps above

Japan Angels 28

In the trough behind the wave

The mouth pulls

Oxygen the body powers through

Japan Angels 29

High walls around them of small jars

Liquid jewels

How their power and brightness heals

Japan Angels 30

A path for the mighty
Guardian
The wind roars through

Japan Angels 31

Caught my eye as I ran by
Looked closer
At thy beauty Marguerite

Japan Angels 32

He held me in his powerful arms

We were yelling

He never got angry as far as we know

Japan Angels 33

Bagged it & smiled me through
Another done
Smiled again & smiled again

Japan Angels 34

Closed my hand about you
Warm joy
Formed a word for you here

Japan Angels 35

Small beneath he struck the cloud

It shouts

My body shakes in its joyful thunder

Japan Angels 36

Wings uplift ascending cranes
Xmas tree
Column teach the truth I need

Japan Angels 37

Eye to eye she peered deep
I am instantly
Mirrored I shine in her eye

Japan Angels 38

Am I really a man or a woman

Less important

More important I am perfectly able

Japan Angels 39

The best lesson I was given

How I felt

When I knew I'd left it at home

Japan Angels 40

Strangely good you walk around

Falling in love

Heartbroken over and over

Japan Angels 41

Sit on the verandah

Let upwell

The true inner core

Japan Angels 42

Under your skirt we beat the chill
Sleepily
Was that your toe I am treading on

Japan Angels 43

Quiet there he is behind the tree

That's his nose

Glowing like a bud of white plum

Japan Angels 44

Accurately describing the form

Discover

A new species a new life to thought

Japan Angels 45

I sat and listened for an hour

Gradually

Dawned on me the light of wisdom

Japan Angels 46

Compacted clouds two naked babes
Push & pull
Far below the people ooh and aah

Japan Angels 47

Call the mountain
Ring the breeze
In the city resound

Japan Angels 48

A valiant strength in your hope
Sings the verse
The love which remains always

Japan Angels 49

Opening now

Star babe

Five pink toes

Japan Angels 50

I would prefer not to lick you
Two dragons
Stand left and right tails touch

Japan Angels 51

Humanity must live within Nature

My dear how true

Defend and guard   a duty for you

Japan Angels 52

Wearing winter plumage

Now viewing

They're breeding in Ueno

Japan Angels 53

Swing the body round the corner
Perfectly
Place the step at the old lady's feet

Japan Angels 54

Please a special request I know I've been slacking

Forgive that

Exercise your powers up there & get me through

Japan Angels 55

Why are we so happy? Look

Pale gold

Good year fruit of the earth

Japan Angels 56

Keep the gifts of dance & song alive
Angel task
Bring a new audience to the show

Japan Angels 57

Wings and eyebrows
White and grey
In sunlight a beacon

Japan Angels 58

Go from a door to an island

Whirl in water

Talk the first days & rejoice

Japan Angels 59

The big one will speak
Good springs here
To the height this way

Japan Angels 60

White & red together

Opened it

She floored me in one

Japan Angels 61

There's a tree with bells

A whispering

Silver-white in the breeze

Japan Angels 62

One for you & one for me

We split them

She took too many & I laughed

Japan Angels 63

Light on the mountain pure white
Cape in gold
Dawn advances the song uprises

Japan Angels 64

Look on the water from the hill

You will see

One walking in the rain and mist

Japan Angels 65

Trundling down the street

Enthroned

Emit a high-pitched song

Japan Angels 66

At the going-in and coming-out
I guard you
By me Japan will not suffer cold

Japan Angels 67

Other-worldly mountain
Under you
We are perfectly warm & safe

Japan Angels 68

Mellow, sweet and fragrant
Met you once
Searching for thee all my life

Japan Angels 69

Future family send me a helper

A take-copter

To my boyhood get me through

Japan Angels 70

Love will make the world weep

Beautiful Life

There'll be no difference there

Japan Angels 71

Choose the best for Japan

I will live

On the shouts of the people

Japan Angels 72

Sweet cherub staring at me

Daring me

Bite my head or tail beware

Japan Angels 73

Wash force through crevice

Brush the rocks

Roar the water-jet in her hand

Japan Angels 74

Hard durance lifting leaden feet
T-shirt drenched
Stand and breathe and take the view

Japan Angels 75

The hot water pours from the faucet

A mighty torrent

Ease the body into the piping heat

Japan Angels 76

Soft & moist in my hands
Push & pull
Dab divide rejoin & rest

Japan Angels 77

Ocean currents build and flow

Wash the shores

Rivers flow like pillars to the sky

Japan Angels 78

Will they be found there

They give

A life a sacrifice of love

Japan Angels 79

Whisper in my finger tips
Beautiful words
Let me sing aloud in joy

Japan Angels 80

Soundlessly the hands dance
Telling a tale
Moved by thee I laugh & cry

Japan Angels 81

Long flight and weary arrival
Home at last
Pour on the boiling let it stand

Japan Angels 82

Crowding into screen Nausicaa

Totoro

Great family you called them to life

Japan Angels 83

I took all my clothes off, wooden bowl
Strategic
Walked into the steam and said friends

Japan Angels 84

Lift up high the fingers go
Salute
Move below the fingers show

Japan Angels 85

Gentle and considerate
Before I knew
I had told her all I'd done

Japan Angels 86

Pushing the limit within
Going beyond
Myself to better myself

Japan Angels 87

Tight or squashy

On a plate

True taste of life

Japan Angels 88

The way the word the life

Soft & gentle

The robe you'll have to wear

Japan Angels 89

A dream-song echoing

Joyful

Heaven in her words

Japan Angels 90

Mukogawa flower anew

Raise

An old skyline of virtue

Japan Angels 91

Hammering the air overhead
Eye
Guard the river smoothly flow

Japan Angels 92

Long white line setting west
Turning orange
Turning red & then the stars

Japan Angels 93

Mirror in the gloss

Lustrous

Gleam the rich black

Japan Angels 94

A ringing voice the shamisen thrum
The curtain fall
Too soon! Rise! Beat drum! Dance on!

Japan Angels 95

Warmth presses on me
We cannot move
Unless the river moves

Japan Angels 96

Clanging a bright red stampede
Riding mighty
Uncoiling a long lithe recoiling

Japan Angels 97

Bells going off bong bong bong bong
Bouncing
The long black-yellow finger says No

Japan Angels 98

Shoveling the black powder
Appearing
In the curtain of dancing flame

Japan Angels 99

Burning three days three nights

Come to birth

The cold black core the pure-bright

Japan Angels 100

The cloth of the sky shaken
In color
Her perfume and her hair

Poem Number and Note

0. Dedication poem: Japan Angel (page 3) 令和。
1. Guardian angels of Japan.
2. Era names 元号 Gengō. 白雉・朱鳥・平成・令和。
3. Emperor Akihito.
4. ランドセル。Elementary school knapsack.
5. Empress Michiko of Japan.
6. Chrysanthemum.
7. Crown Prince Naruhito.
8. Mount Fuji.
9. Hiragana.
10. Kyoto.
11. 石清水八幡宮・節分。Iwashimizu Hachimangu, Yawata. Setsubun.
12. Rollercoaster Japan.
13. 東大寺二月堂・お水取り・奈良市。Tōdaiji Nigatsudō Omizutori. Nara.
14. 東大寺・奈良市。Niō, Tōdaiji Temple gate, Nara.
15. Librarian.
16. 日本郵便箱。Mailbox.
17. JDF Naval officer.
18. Kabuki & Takarazuka dance.
19. JDF Ground auxiliary rescue.
20. 和菓子。Wagashi (sweetmeat).
21. Kanadehon Chūshingura 大星由良助。Ōboshi Yuranosuke.
22. Letter.
23. Pilgrim.
24. JDF Navy cadets.
25. Staff nurse.
26. 能面・逆髪・大宮大和真盛作・香雪美術館神戸。Noh Mask.
27. JDF Fighter.
28. Inspired by swimming ace 池江璃花子 Ikee Rikako.
29. 日本薬局。Pharmacist.
30. Shinkansen.
31. Marguerite Daisy. Cp SM365.1.376-393.
32. Psychiatric nurse.
33. レジ。On the till.

34. 握り寿司・結び。Nigiri-zushi, musubi.
35. 和太鼓。Wadaiko.
36. 薬師寺東塔。Yakushiji Higashi Tō, Nara.
37. Optician.
38. High-Achiever.
39. 弁当箱。Bentobako. Lunch box.
40. 渥美清、Atsumi Kiyoshi, Torasan. "Otoko wa Tsurai Yo" Yamada Yōji film-series (1969-1995).
41. 南禅寺。Nanzenji, Kyoto.
42. Kotatsu with well.
43. 天狗。Tengu.
44. Scientific method.
45. Buddhist sermon.
46. 相撲。Sumo.
47. Bells.
48. 敬宮・愛子内親王。Princess Toshi, Aiko-sama.
49. Sakura blossom.
50. 郵便切手。First Postage Stamps Japan 1871.
51. 「人は自然界の中で生きている」秋篠宮悠仁・12歳。
52. Ptarmigan. Lagopus mutus breeding programs in Ueno Zoo.
53. Kyoto bus driver.
54. 天神。Tenjin. 菅原道眞 Sugawara Michizane, deity of passing exams.
55. タケノコ。Take no ko.
56. 五代目坂東玉三郎 Bandō Tamasaburō "Amaterasu."
57. Himeji castle.
58. 明石海峡大橋。Akashi Ōhashi. Akashi Bridge.
59. 日本人氏名。[富士山・比叡山]。Puzzle for 山口。
60. 김치。Kimchi.
61. 日本人氏名。鈴・篤・薄。Puzzle for 鈴木。
62. 明石焼き。Akashi-yaki.
63. 北海道。Japan-Russian Orthodox.
64. 琵琶湖。Lake Biwa.
65. Electric wheelchair.
66. Surgical mask.
67. Roof.
68. 日本茶玉露。Japanese green tea gyokuro.
69. Doraemon.
70. TV Drama *Beautiful Life* TBS 2000 木村拓哉 Kimura Takuya, 常盤貴子 Tokiwa Takako.
71. Japanese democracy.

72. たい焼き。Taiyaki.
73. Dental nurse.
74. Climbing 大文字山。Daimonji in July.
75. Japanese bathtub.
76. Swan Bakery.
77. Chant. 永平寺。Eiheiji Zazen; 北海道灯台の聖母修道院。St Benedict Gregorian.
78. Labrador guide-dog.
79. Japanese Braille.
80. Japanese Sign Language.
81. Nissin Cup Noodles.
82. 宮崎駿 Miyazaki Hayao & Ghibli team.
83. 銭湯 Sentō (traditional bathhouse).
84. Hand signals.
85. Japanese policewoman.
86. Inspired by 鈴木一朗 Suzuki Ichiro baseball retirement speech (20190321).
87. 梅干。Umeboshi.
88. 柔道着。Judogi (Judo sportswear).
89. Uguisu. Japanese bush warbler.
90. 尼崎城天守再建 Amagasaki Castle rebuilt (March 2019).
91. Helicopter.
92. Vapor trail.
93. 輪島塗。Wajima lacquer.
94. 日本舞踊。北野をどり。Kitano odori. Traditional dance.
95. 四条通八坂神社 New Year's Eve Yasaka Jinja, Kyoto (1986).
96. 消防自動車。Fire-engine.
97. 踏切。Fumikiri. Level crossing.
98. 島根県奥出雲町・はがね。Smelting with a traditional tatara furnace.
99. Shimane Okuizumo-cho making 鋼 hagane, best-quality steel for swords.
100. 花火。Fireworks.

Profile

Stean Anthony

I'm British, based in Japan. I've written a series of books of poetry promoting understanding and peace. Find out more from the list at the end of this book. I have also published *Eco-Friendly Japan*, Eihosha, Tokyo (2008). *Monday Songs 1-7,* and *Eitanka 1* (pdf file textbook freely available on website – and sound files). Thanks to Yamaguchi MK for kind help.

Forthcoming

Enarchae (story in short paragraphs)

Hagios Paulos 4 (songs on the theme of Saint Paul)

Hana Book 2 (verses on theme of flowers & other things)

Heiankyō Book 2 (translations of classic Japanese poetry)

Saint Mark 452 (translation of Gospel into Japanese verses)

Saint Mary 365 book 7 (verses dedicated to the BVM)

Sport book 2 (verses on the theme of sport)

Author's profits to be divided into three between:

One Shinto Shrine Ise Jingu, Ise (dating back more than 2000 years)

One Buddhist Temple Todaiji Temple, Nara (c. 750 CE)

One Christian Church 大浦天主堂 Ōura Tenshudō Church, Nagasaki (1865) to share 50% with Nikolai-do, Holy Resurrection Cathedral, Chiyoda, Tokyo (1891) and other churches.

Stean Anthony Books with Yamaguchi Shoten. Original poetry & translations & adaptations. Most are textbooks.

- *Selections from Shakespeare 1-5* (selected passages)
- *Great China 1-4* (translations of classical Chinese poetry)
- *Kŏngzĭ 136* (poems based on the sayings of Confucius)
- *Manyōshū 365* (translations of ancient Japanese poems)
- *One Hundred Poems* (inspired by 百人一首 *Hyakunin Isshu*)
- *Heiankyō 1* (translations of ancient Japanese poems)
- *Inorijuzu* (Buddhist & Christian words for peace)
- *Sufisongs* (poems for peace in Jerusalem)
- *Soulsongs* (poems for peace in Jerusalem)
- *Pashsongs* (songs & poems by Stean Anthony)
- *Bird* (poems on the theme of birds)
- *Sport* (poems on the theme of sport)
- *Hana 1* (poems on the theme of flowers)
- *Songs 365* (poems based on the Psalms)
- *Songs 365* (Japanese translation)
- *Songs for Islam* (poems based on verses in the Koran)
- *Isaiah Isaiah Bright Voice* (poems inspired by Bk of Isaiah)
- *Saint Paul 200* (poetic phrases from the *Letters of Paul*)
- *Hagios Paulos 1-3* (poetry based on life & letters of St Paul)
- *Gospel 365* (based on the Synoptic Gospels)
- *Saint John 550* (poetic version of the Gospel of St John)
- *Saint John 391* (translation to Japanese of *Saint John 550*)

- *Saint John 190* (transl. to Japanese of *Saint John 550* Catholic Letters)
- *Saint Matthew 331* (poetic version of Gospel of St Matthew)
- *Saint Luke 132* (chaps 1-2 in Japanese verse *"Mary's Gospel"*)
- *Saint Mary 100* (poems dedicated to St Mary)
- *Saint Mary 365 Books 1-6* (calendar of poems on themes relating to Mary, Holy Mother, flowers, icons, prayer, scripture)

- *Messages to My Mother 1-7* (essays on faith and other things)
- *Mozzicone 1-2* (essays about questions of faith & other things)
- *Monday Songs 1-7* (pdf textbooks of English songs)
- *Eitanka 1* (pdf textbook teaching poetry)
- *Psalms in English* (75+ lectures in English teaching the Psalms pdf textbook). Pdf are freely available.
- *Piesat Course 1-3 Lectures on English Poetry* (pdf text files)

- *Exnihil* (story written in short paragraphs)
- *Barešitbara* (story written in short paragraphs)

JAPAN ANGELS
by Stean Anthony

Company : Yamaguchi Shoten
Address : 4-2 Kamihate-cho, Kitashirakawa
Sakyo-ku, Kyoto, 606-8252
Japan
Tel. 075-781-6121
Fax. 075-705-2003

JAPAN ANGELS　　　　　　定価 本体1,000円（税別）

2019年11月20日 初　版

著　者　Stean　Anthony
発行者　山 口 ケイコ
印刷所　大村印刷株式会社
発行所　株式会社　山口書店
〒606-8252京都市左京区北白川上終町4-2
TEL：075-781-6121　FAX：075-705-2003
出張所電話　福岡092-713-8575

ISBN 978-4-8411-0944-3　C1182
©2019 Stean Anthony